# DINOSAUR Land

## The Magic FOSSIL

## M.J.MISRA

EGMONT

For Luca, who had the idea.

Love Mum, who wrote it for you.

# EGMONT

*We bring stories to life*

*Dinosaur Land: The Magic Fossil*
First published in Great Britain 2012
by Egmont UK Limited
239 Kensington High Street
London W8 6SA

ISBN 978 1 4052 5877 7

1 3 5 7 9 10 8 6 4 2

www.egmont.co.uk

A CIP catalogue record for this title is available from the British Library

Printed and bound by CPI Group (UK) Ltd, Croydon, CR0 4YY

49121/3

## EGMONT LUCKY COIN

# CONTENTS

# The Magic Fossil

'Come on, Max!' Mr Jordan called. 'It's time to go home!'

Max glanced up. His mum and dad had started walking slowly back along the pebble beach towards the car park. But surely he still had time to explore for a few more minutes? Crouching down, he sifted through the stones with his fingers, looking for fossils to add to his collection. He loved fossils almost as much as he loved dinosaurs! And that was saying something . . .

Max had been dinosaur-mad for as long as he could remember. Every night, when his mum came in to read him a bedtime story, Max wanted his dinosaur fact book. He knew it off by heart! The biggest dinosaurs were called sauropods and the dinosaurs that had the most teeth were hadrosaurs and the dinosaur with the longest tail was the diplodocus.

'Max!' Mrs Jordan called, looking over her shoulder. 'We'll go without you!'

'Coming!' Max gave a sigh. It didn't seem like he would find a fossil that day. But as he stood up, something pale and grey caught his eye. It looked just like a snail's shell.

Max swooped down. It was an ammonite fossil! He sucked in an excited breath – this fossil must be millions of years old!

As Max traced the fossil's spiral shell with his fingers, he felt a strange tingle run up his arms. He decided it must have been the sea breeze, and ran after his mum and dad, his feet slipping slightly on the stones. They had reached the Land Rover and his mum was unlocking it.

His dad smiled. 'Did you find a fossil?'

'Yes, look!' Max held it out.

'Wow! That's a beauty!' Mr Jordan said. 'Definitely one for your collection.'

Max got into the Land Rover, his feet jostling for space on the floor with leaflets about animal care, an empty bottle of horse medicine and a box of flea tablets for dogs. His mum and dad were both vets in the small town of Little Hadley.

'Fish and chips for tea tonight, Max?' Mrs Jordan asked as she started the engine.

'Yes please!' said Max happily. It was one of his favourites! His tummy rumbled as the car moved forwards.

Mr Jordan looked over his shoulder, his blue eyes twinkling. 'What does a giant tyrannosaurus eat for tea then, Max?'

Max grinned. He knew the answer to that one. 'Anything he wants!'

After tea, Max helped his mum check on the animals that were staying in the surgery overnight, while his dad went off on his rounds to see a newborn calf. The mother cow had died quite soon after the calf had been born, so it had been a tricky time. But Max's dad had placed the calf with another cow – a foster mother – and it looked like they were finally settling in together.

After checking on the animals, Max got into bed and his mum came and sat with him. Together they looked at the dinosaur fact book. 'Test me!' Max begged his mum.

She shook her head. 'You know the answer to every question, Max.'

'It doesn't matter . . . let's do them again!'

'OK, just one,' Mrs Jordan said, looking through the book. 'What dinosaur was about nine metres long and about three metres tall, had a long spiky tail and spiny plates of armour on its back?'

'Too easy, Mum! It's a stegosaurus!' The stegosaurus was one of Max's favourite dinosaurs. It looked big and scary but it was a plant-eater and was gentle and friendly unless it was being attacked.

'Bedtime now.' Mrs Jordan kissed Max on

the forehead. 'Night, Dinosaur Boy.'

'Night, Mum.' Max snuggled down under

his dinosaur duvet cover. His mum went to

the door and turned out the light.

'Mum?'

'Yes?'

Max propped himself up on his elbows. 'What do you call a dinosaur that left its armour out in the rain?'

'Hmmm. I don't know.'

'A stegosaur-rust!' said Max with a grin.

'Oh, Max!' Mrs Jordan shook her head and smiled as she shut the door.

Max lay there in the dark, running his hands slowly over the book that was lying on his bed. He looked over at his fossil collection, on the shelves above his chest of drawers. His new fossil was there, right at the front. Max suddenly felt a strange urge to pick it up. Getting out of bed, he padded over and took the fossil down from the shelf. His fingers began to trace the outline of the spiral as he got back into bed. Just think, when this fossil was alive, dinosaurs had been alive too! They'd walked the Earth – stegosaurus, tyrannosaurus, triceratops . . .

Oh, I wish I could meet a dinosaur, Max thought with all his heart. Just at that moment he felt a tingle run over his hand, like a gentle buzz of electricity. He blinked. The fossil suddenly looked very different. A pale light was shining from it, out into the room.

Max almost dropped the fossil in shock. 'Wh-what?' he stammered as the light grew brighter and a humming noise began to fill the air. Max opened his mouth to yell for

his mum, but just as
he did so, a whoosh
of colours swirled all
around him.

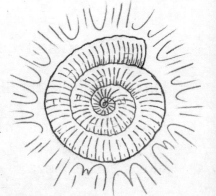

'Whoa!' Max cried as he was
slowly lifted up. It was like being caught in a
whirlwind! He span and rolled and twisted,
as if he was on a mad rollercoaster. His
fingers clutched the fossil. All he could see
were the swirling colours . . . then, suddenly,
he landed with a bump on hard ground.

Max rubbed his eyes as the colours vanished. The first thing he felt was the sun on his skin. His mouth dropped open as he stared around him. He wasn't in his bedroom any more. He'd landed in some kind of desert, and a very hot and dusty one at that. Craggy rocks and boulders lay scattered everywhere and far in the distance he could just make out a lake, shimmering in the strong sunlight.

'What's going on?' he gasped.

# Under Attack!

Max got to his feet and turned all around. The sky was blue and hazy and the sun beat down. In the distance, he could see a mountain – no, hang on, not just any mountain . . . a smoking mountain. It had to be a volcano! And over to his right there was a thick wood of enormous trees.

Was this a dream? Had he fallen asleep? Max looked down and saw that he was still in his pyjamas. But it didn't feel like a dream. A haze of large black insects was buzzing around his head. He felt a sting as one of them bit him. It was most definitely not a dream!

'Ow!' Max swatted the insects away. He wiped his hand across his face. Wherever he was, it was extremely hot. He needed to find some shade.

He headed towards the trees, taking another look around him as he walked. It was an incredible place. He could just see what looked like a herd of deer grazing at the lake's edge. Butterflies flew from stone to stone and insects hummed gently. It was like being in a wildlife

programme or stepping into a nature book. He'd never been anywhere like this before.

Max was so lost in his thoughts that he nearly didn't notice the flock of birds flying out of the woods. They swooped and swayed, chasing each other through the skies.

Max rubbed his eyes. Wait a minute! That couldn't be right. The birds had furry bodies and leathery wings and, as they flew closer, he could see that they were massive. Their beaks were long and razor-sharp.

'Pterodactyls!' he gasped as one of them opened its beak and let out a shrieking cry.

He looked over at the animals by the lake again, straining his eyes. Suddenly he realised that they were no ordinary deer. The animals were green and brown with long, thin back legs, shorter front legs and long, stiff tails. 'Dryosaurus . . .' he breathed.

Max stopped dead. Dinosaurs! He was

in a place with dinosaurs! Fear flashed quickly through him, then a massive rush of excitement. This was amazing! He didn't know how it had happened or where he was, but his wish had come true and he was finally seeing actual, real dinosaurs!

Max broke into a run for the trees. When he got there he screeched to a halt as he saw yet another dinosaur – a gigantic brachiosaurus – stripping the leaves off the top branches. Max nearly laughed out loud

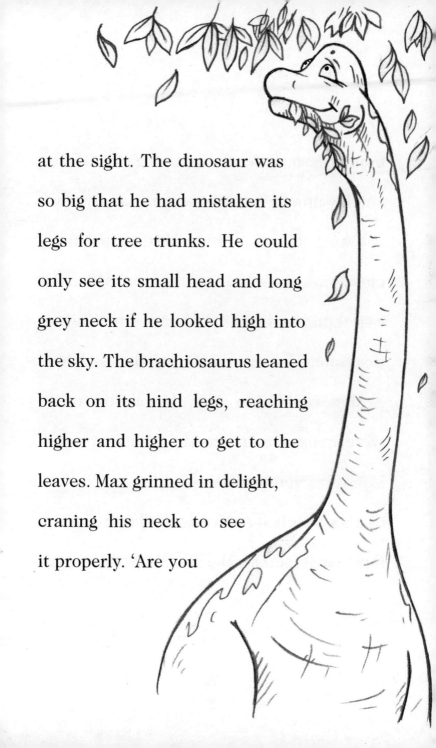

at the sight. The dinosaur was so big that he had mistaken its legs for tree trunks. He could only see its small head and long grey neck if he looked high into the sky. The brachiosaurus leaned back on its hind legs, reaching higher and higher to get to the leaves. Max grinned in delight, craning his neck to see it properly. 'Are you enjoying your dinner up there?' he called.

The brachiosaurus stopped, as if it was listening to Max. But as Max looked more closely, he could see the dinosaur was twitching its head back and forth. It was distracted by something in the distance! And now, by the lake, the dryosauruses were making a trumpeting, braying noise. What was going on?

Max watched as the flock of pterodactyls flew back across the sky, cawing loudly.

Something was definitely happening . . .

And then Max heard another noise – a thundering, pounding sound, like galloping horse hooves, getting closer and closer. He span round in a panic, just in time to see a very large, very round dinosaur hurtling across the plain. It was heading straight towards him!

Max froze in shock. The dinosaur's head was lowered in the attack position. The ground was shaking. It was only thirty metres away . . . now twenty. It was going to flatten him!

RUN! Max's brain screamed. Then, *no*. Don't panic. Think.

Max knew from his parents that the worst thing you could do if an animal charged at you was to run away.

Now that he was calmer, he could see the dinosaur clearly. It had heavy, armoured plates and a spiny tail. As it hurtled forwards, its brick-red spines banged up and down.

Max knew this type of dinosaur, and he knew there was nothing to be scared of. Some instinct made him step forwards and he held out his hand.

'Gently now, boy. Easy does it,' he murmured.

For a moment, Max really did think the dinosaur was going to run him down but, at the very last minute, the beast swerved to one side and skidded to a halt. Max stayed very still. He suddenly felt smaller than he had ever done in his life. His head only came up to the top of the dinosaur's leg! It was like standing next to a fully grown elephant.

The dinosaur slowly turned its head back to look at him. Max swallowed, his skin prickly and his heart thumping so loud he could almost hear it.

'Hello,' he whispered as he gazed at the massive

stegosaurus. He continued to hold out his hand. What was the dinosaur going to do?

The stegosaurus lifted its nose to Max's face and snuffled.

Max couldn't help himself. 'That tickles!' he laughed as the whiskery jaw of the dinosaur whispered over his face and then down to his hand.

The dinosaur breathed in and out and then stared at Max again. Cautiously, Max reached out and touched its face with his other hand. Its orangey-red skin felt rough and bumpy. Max stroked it and the dinosaur let out a deep, happy sigh.

'That's incredible!'

Max span round. A girl, about his own age, was jogging towards him. She was dressed in furs, draped over one shoulder and held in place by some sort of clip. She had dark

curly hair and she was
barefoot like Max.

Max stared at her.
'Who are you?'

'I'm Fern,' the girl said.
She stopped a little way
from the dinosaur and
looked at Max excitedly.
'And who are you?'

'I . . . I'm Max,' said Max.
'Where am I?'

'You really don't know?' asked Fern.

Max shook his head and patted the stegosaurus as it nuzzled him.

Fern grinned. 'You're in Dinosaur Land!'

# Back at the House

'Dinosaur Land?' Max gulped.

'Come and sit down and I'll explain,' said Fern.

Max gave the stegosaurus a goodbye pat and then joined Fern on a rock, near to where the brachiosaurus was munching again at the leaves. They didn't go too close, but leaves and twigs still fell down on their heads as Fern started to talk.

'Every time a dinosaur became extinct in the human world it came to live here,' she explained. 'There are loads and loads of dinosaurs in Dinosaur Land.'

Max's eyes widened in amazement. 'I've come from the human world too,' he said. 'I hope I'm not extinct, though!' He told Fern how the fossil on the beach had transported him to Dinosaur Land. It all sounded kind

of crazy, even to his own ears.

'Oh, wow!' gasped Fern. 'So magic brought you to us! I wonder why?' She shrugged. 'Whatever the reason, you should come and meet my dad. I'm sure he'd really like to meet *you*. We never have visitors! He looks out for any sick and injured dinosaurs in Dinosaur Land and I help him. We live just over there.' She pointed into the distance. 'You know, you were really brave not to run from that stegosaurus.'

'I nearly did,' admitted Max. 'But then I realised what kind of dinosaur it was. I know stegosauruses eat plants and there was no reason for it to eat something as tasteless as me! I also remembered what my mum and dad always say – never, ever run from a charging animal. They're vets, you see.'

'Vets?' Fern looked puzzled.

'Vets are people who care for animals in my world,' explained Max. 'A bit like your dad does here.'

Max raised his hand for a high five but Fern didn't seem to know what to do. She reached out and tried to shake his hand instead. They looked at each other and both giggled. 'I can't believe this is really happening!' said Max.

'And I can't believe you're really here. It'll be brilliant,' said Fern. 'Let's go and see my Dad. I want to see his face when he notices your weird clothes!'

'*My* weird clothes!' Max exclaimed, looking down at his pyjamas. 'What about yours?'

They grinned at each other and started walking across the plain.

'Well, whether your clothes are weird or not, you can borrow some from us while you're here,' said Fern. 'Now, come on, I bet you we'll find my dad with Cory.'

'Cory?' asked Max.

'He's an allosaurus,' said Fern. 'He's staying with us at the moment.'

'He's staying with you?' Max looked shocked as he thought about his fact book and pictured the two-legged dinosaur with its long neck and tail. It was a meat-eater that ran fast on two legs and had very strong, sharp teeth.

'Don't worry, Cory's just a baby,' Fern

laughed, seeing Max's worried expression.
'I know he's a meat-eater but he won't hurt
you. He's only two weeks old.' A sad look
crossed her face. 'He's not doing too well at
the moment. We only found him last week.
He was wandering about on his own, hungry
and thirsty, and his mother was missing.'

'Poor thing,' Max said.

Fern nodded. 'We've been trying to nurse
him back to health, but he's not happy.
Maybe you can help us – after all, you seem

to know quite a bit about dinosaurs.'

'I'll try!' promised Max.

It was a long walk across the plain but at last they reached a winding, dusty path marked with a white boulder. A pale stone house stood at the end, with four openings for windows. Simple and plain, it looked inviting all the same.

As they walked round the corner of the house, Max was in for a surprise.

'Look at all those dinosaurs!' he breathed, as lots of different creatures called out to them from inside large paddocks. Some were feeding, some were splashing in pools of water – but they all looked as though they were having fun.

Fern beckoned Max over to a little barn at the end of a path. 'This is where Cory lives.'

They went inside. It was so dark that it took a while for Max's eyes to adjust, then he saw a man standing in front of them.

He had the same dark, curly hair as Fern
and was stroking a very young dinosaur.
It was just a bit smaller than Max, with
greeny-brown skin and
red stripes on its back.

'Dad,' said Fern. 'This
is Max. I found him
out on the reserve.'

She quickly explained what had happened.

Her dad looked amazed. 'A visitor from the human world? How astonishing! I've never known anyone visit us from there before. I wonder why you've been brought here?' Fern's dad shook his head, his brown eyes smiling. 'Well, whatever the reason, it's good to meet you, Max. I'm Adam. Did Fern tell you about Cory?'

'She did,' said Max. 'It's awful.'

'It's certainly not looking good,' Adam

agreed, frowning sadly at the baby dinosaur in front of him. 'And he's worse today. He's refusing to eat anything – even the dragonflies and centipedes he usually loves.'

'Oh, yes, they like insects when they're tiny, don't they?' said Max, peering at the little creature.

'That's right,' said Fern. 'It's quite a treat for them.'

'He's become so quiet,' said Adam. 'I've tried everything, but nothing has worked.

If things carry on like this, he's not going to survive. I wish I knew what we could do.'

Max looked at the allosaurus. He knew that he would grow much bigger but, right now, with his wide, sad eyes, he was as sweet as a little foal.

'Do you have any ideas, Max?' Fern asked.

Max thought hard. He moved closer to the baby dinosaur, crouched down and held out his hand. Oh, if only he could help, before it was too late . . .

# A Brave Plan

The little allosaurus snuffled at Max and then pulled away. Max wondered what his mum and dad would do in this situation. He remembered what they'd been doing that very day. *What if . . .*

No, it was just a silly idea – it might work with ordinary animals but it would never work with a dinosaur. Or would it?

'You know, maybe there *is* something,' Max said, feeling a bit more confident as he saw Adam and Fern's eyes light up. 'At home, Mum and Dad have been treating a sick calf who lost her mother. The calf wouldn't take any food and was pining away. My parents put her with another cow who had recently given birth but had lost her own calf too . . . and, well, within days the sick calf was feeding again.'

'It's a good idea, Max,' Adam said gently. 'But I'm afraid we've tried it already – with Rosie, a triceratops whose babies hatched out of their eggs just days ago. Sadly, Rosie didn't respond to Cory and in the end she rejected him.'

'If anything, it made matters worse,' Fern went on. 'That's when Cory started refusing his food.' She leaned into the little allosaurus with a handful of insects. 'Here, boy, just take a few,' she said.

But Cory only pushed her away. 'You see,' said Fern, tears welling up in her eyes. 'Nothing works and if we don't do something soon, he could die!'

Max felt terrible. Surely there had to be a way of making his idea work. He wracked his brain . . . and suddenly something came to him. What if Rosie was simply the wrong dinosaur to place Cory with?

'Hang on,' Max started. 'You said Rosie was a triceratops – a plant-eater – right?

But Cory's a meat-eater.'

'Yes,' said Adam, looking surprised. 'So?'

'So maybe that's the answer!' Max said excitedly. 'Maybe Cory needs a meat-eater as a foster mum?'

Fern looked hopefully at her dad.

'I don't know,' said Adam. 'Even if that were the case, it's not going to help us. We haven't got another meat-eating dinosaur here.'

'Oh,' said Max, all his excitement fading.

As he looked over at the little allosaurus, settling down miserably into the corner of his pen, he felt very sad. Time was slipping away, and fast.

'Come on, Max,' said Fern, touching his arm. 'Let's go and get you those clothes I promised, then I'll show you around. Cory needs some rest.'

Max didn't want to leave the little dinosaur but he knew there was nothing more he could do for now. He followed Fern into the whitewashed house. It was nice and cool inside and Max was glad for a chance to sit down on a stone chair. Fern started to pull some clothes out of a chest on the floor.

'How about this?' she asked, holding up a long fur tunic, similar to the one she was wearing.

Max laughed as he pulled it on and tied it with the leather cord Fern handed him. It felt kind of funny but at least it made him fit in better in Dinosaur Land. He suddenly

felt a bit happier.

'Come on then,' he said. 'What about that

tour you offered me?'

'All right!' Fern grinned, dragging him

back out into the daylight. 'Let's go.'

As the two of them walked outside, they passed a muddy old swamp filled with clumps of small trees.

'What's that over there?' Max pointed to a pen all on its own, some way away from the other paddocks.

'That's the contagious pen,' said Fern, 'where dinosaurs go if they have an illness the other dinosaurs could catch.'

Max nodded. It was similar to how his

parents worked in the human world. They also separated off any animals that might be a danger to the others.

As they passed different paddocks, Fern told Max about the dinosaurs inside them. 'This is Jody,' she said, coming to a halt next to a deer-like dinosaur with a red frill on the top of her head. 'She's a lambeosaurus. She had an open wound – probably from a fight with another dinosaur. The wound was infected so we've been treating it with bandages infused with herbs. Hopefully she'll be better in a few days.'

As if on cue, the dinosaur let out a little bleating sound, like a sheep, and both Max and Fern laughed.

'Just like her name,' said Fern.

'She *so* doesn't sound scary,' said Max.

'Plant-eaters aren't scary,' said Fern. 'They're really gentle creatures. We usually only treat plant-eaters or young meat-eaters at the house because adult meat-eaters are just too dangerous. They always try to break free and eat all the other dinosaurs. If Dad treats meat-eaters he does it away from here.'

They moved on to the next enclosure where a colourful parasaurolophus stood.

'He's got a broken bone,' Fern explained. 'His pack rejected him. Once the bone is set we'll work on building his strength so that he can rejoin them back in the wild.' They moved on to the next enclosure. 'And here are Rosie and her hatchlings.'

Max looked over the fencing and saw an enormous porcupine-shaped dinosaur with a round tummy, a long tail and three horns, sheltering her two babies under the trees.

'Wow!' Max was amazed by the size of her. 'She looks just like a rhino, only much bigger.'

'Triceratops can be dangerous in the wild if they feel threatened,' Fern explained. 'One swipe of that tail and she could take out a pretty large predator, and her horns would spear right through them.'

Looking at the gentle giant in front of him now, caring for her young, Max found it hard to believe. The baby triceratops nuzzled into their mother and she let out a contented sigh.

'Look how she's feeding them,' said Fern as Rosie reached into the tree and munched on a mouthful of leaves before passing them down to her pups.

Max could see why Adam and Fern had thought she would be the right fit for Cory – she was the perfect mother.

Poor Cory . . . if only there was someone out there for him too. Max thought hard. The seed of an idea began to bounce around in his mind. OK, so the perfect foster dinosaur

might not be right here near the house but, out there, in the depths of the forest, there had to be loads of meat-eating dinosaurs. Surely one of them would take on the job of being Cory's mum?

'I've had a thought,' Max said, turning slowly to Fern. 'About helping Cory. What if we could get a meat-eater somewhere else? From out in the wild.'

'But we'd have to go out there and look for one,' said Fern, shocked. 'It would be far too dangerous.'

'But we can't sit here and do nothing,' Max protested. 'I'm not saying we have to bring back a big one like a T-Rex, but how about a smaller one – like a dryptosaurus or a raptor?'

'Hmm.' Fern looked thoughtful. 'A smaller dinosaur might work. Maybe it wouldn't be that dangerous.'

'Most small meat-eaters work in packs, don't they?' said Max. 'That will make it difficult, but we could try to find one that's on its own.'

'How would we get it to come here?' Fern asked.

'The dinosaur eggs!' said Max. 'The ones that Rosie's babies hatched from. Would you have kept the shells?'

'I think so,' Fern said uncertainly. 'They'd probably be in Rosie's enclosure.'

'So, we could lay a trail. A meat-eating dinosaur would be sure to scent out the egg shells and think they'd find a weak or abandoned hatchling at the end.'

'It might work,' said Fern. 'Dad would never agree to it . . . but maybe, just maybe, we could do it on our own. We could slip out without him noticing.'

Max looked at Fern. Fern looked back at him and grinned.

'I think we have a plan!' she said.

# out in the wild

Max and Fern crept down the winding track
that led away from the little white house.

'It is a good plan, isn't it?' Max whispered.

Fern nodded. 'We have to do something,
for Cory's sake. We can't just watch him die!
Come on, let's hurry before Dad sees us.'

'You've got the shells?' Max asked.

Fern nodded. She had a leather bag on her shoulder. 'They're in here.'

As they stepped off the beaten track, Max felt a shiver of excitement run through him. The lake up ahead was glistening. He took a deep breath, soaking in the atmosphere. 'Where should we start?' he asked.

'Let's head for the trees,' said Fern, then she stopped suddenly. 'Shush, look! There, ahead of you!'

Max let out a low whistle at the sight

before him. A slim female dinosaur stood in the clearing, raising herself up on her hind legs and sniffing the air. She was reddish brown from head to toe, with a double crest on the top of her head and short, stubby teeth, giving her an almost crocodile-like appearance.

'A dilophosaurus,' Max breathed. 'That's a meat-eating dinosaur. She must be quite young as she's not very big. She would be perfect! Don't let her see us.'

'So what should we do?' whispered Fern.

'Start laying the egg shells in a trail back towards the house,' said Max. 'Just like we talked about.'

As quietly as they could, Max and Fern retraced their steps, dropping bits of the

dinosaur shells all the way back to the little white boulder that marked the entrance to Fern's home.

'Now we should lay the shells off to the left,' whispered Max. 'We'll lead the dilophosaurus to the contagious pen so that she's far enough away from the plant-eaters and doesn't upset them.'

'Good plan,' said Fern.

'Let's wait here, behind this bush,' said Max, beckoning her over once all the shells were laid. 'We can check that she picks up the scent.'

'But what if she smells us out first?' said Fern, a worried expression on her face.

'We've got to hope she's more tempted by the shells and the smell of her own kind,' said Max. 'All we can do is wait . . .'

Fern pushed back the green leaves of the bush for what seemed like the millionth time. 'Nothing. She hasn't budged an inch.'

'I bet it won't be much longer,' said Max. 'We just need the wind to change – then she'll smell the shells on the breeze.' He saw Fern's face. 'OK, look, how about we tell some jokes while we're waiting?'

Fern groaned as she settled back down on the ground. It was getting cold outside and she was feeling numb from sitting still for so long.

'So, where do prehistoric reptiles like to go on holiday?' Max started.

'I don't know,' muttered Fern.

'To the dino-shore,' Max laughed. 'Get it?'

The corners of Fern's mouth twitched.

'OK, so that one wasn't very good,' Max said. 'Here's another. What do you call a –'

But he didn't have a chance to finish, as Fern placed a hand on his arm to silence him. 'Shush,' she hissed, her eyes wide. 'Look! The dilophosaurus is coming!'

'What?' said Max, spinning round. He didn't know whether to be excited or scared by the sight that greeted him. Sure enough, in the distance, the dinosaur had pricked up her nose. She had definitely smelled something. And now she was heading out of

the clearing, following the trail of egg shells towards them.

'It's working!' Max hissed excitedly.

For a moment, it looked as if the dinosaur had heard something. She stopped and twisted her head round, looking into the distance. But then she was off again, trotting along the trail.

Once more she stopped. But this time it didn't seem to be a noise that had distracted her. She snuffled around, swinging her head from side to side. It was as though she was smelling something nearby – and not in the direction of the contagious pen.

'Uh-oh,' said Fern, nudging Max urgently. 'I . . . I think she might just have picked up our scent . . .'

Max gulped as the dilophosaurus looked straight at the bush they were hiding behind. Then she began to stalk in their direction. Maybe this hadn't been such a good plan after all!

# Disaster!

Max swallowed. 'We have to get her back on the right trail,' he said, pointing towards the pen. 'Come on. Quietly as we can.'

Max and Fern crept from the undergrowth, walking backwards as they watched the dilophosaurus stop and swing her head from side to side. She was clearly trying to find whatever she had smelled before. Her small, dark eyes hadn't spotted them yet.

Max's heart pounded. It'll be OK, he told himself. As long as we're quiet, we should be able to make it down the path. Then we'll be out of her way and she'll pick up the scent of the eggs again.

Carefully, step by step, Max and Fern made their way back, keeping an eye on the dilophosaurus who stood rigid, her nostrils twitching as she scanned the area.

They only had about fifty yards to go . . . now twenty . . . but suddenly it was all too much for Fern and she turned and ran. 'Quick!' she cried back to Max.

Max held out his hand to stop her, but he was too late. It was just the sign the dilophosaurus needed and she charged across the sand. Max made a quick decision. He would have to follow Fern, or he'd be eaten alive! He dashed into the house after Fern, and she slammed the door shut.

'What's going on?' Fern's father was in there, a puzzled look on his face. But he didn't need to ask anything more. The noise outside was enough to tell him something was wrong, and he marched to the door.

'No, Dad! Don't open it! Please!' gasped Fern, dragging him to the window. 'Look!'

Max joined them. Outside, the meat-eating dinosaur was charging around the enclosures with a frightening ROOOOAAAAAAR! The plant-eating dinosaurs looked terrified at the sight of a predator in their midst, and were starting to panic.

A furious Adam turned to Fern and Max.

'I . . . we . . .' stammered Max, but a loud crash from outside stopped him.

They looked out of the window again and could see immediately what had caused the noise. The lambeosaurus had broken out of her pen and was letting out a loud, scared bleating noise.

'We were trying to lead the dilophosaurus

to the pen for really sick dinosaurs,' Max
said helplessly. 'But it didn't quite work out
like that.'

'The contagious pen?' Adam stood by the
door. 'But why?'

'We . . . we . . .' Max stuttered. 'We thought that if we got her here, she might help Cory . . . she might be her foster mother.'

'How did you manage to lure her here?' asked Adam.

'With Rosie's egg shells,' Fern replied.

Adam groaned. 'She followed the scent?'

'Yes,' said Max, looking back outside. 'Only not to the right area.'

'All right, try not to panic.' Adam laid a hand on the children's arms. 'I'm going to have to go out there and settle things down. Just stay here . . .'

Max and Fern watched from the house as Adam rushed outside. There were tears in Fern's brown eyes. Then an even more terrible sight greeted them. Cory! He was out of his pen and heading straight for the dilophosaurus. He must have smelled that she was a meat-eater and thought she was his mother.

The dilophosaurus bucked and swayed

ROOAA

on her two legs as little Cory approached. She gnashed her teeth and let out a savage roar.

Max and Fern held their breath. Adam stopped to the side of the dinosaurs and Cory skidded to a halt with a frightened, high-pitched whine. He started to turn back.

'He's heading for the swamp!' cried Fern. The dilophosaurus gave chase, looking like she wanted to eat Cory, not mother him!

RR!

And then, with a splosh and a splash, Cory dived straight in to the swamp, leaving the dilophosaurus roaring on the side.

'Well done, Cory!' cried Fern.

'Look,' Max pointed. 'The dilophosaurus isn't going to follow him in.'

He let out a relieved sigh as the predator turned her back on the little allosaurus and faced the other dinosaurs, who were all running for cover. Then Max's blood ran cold. The dilophosaurus had spotted the baby triceratops and she was staring straight at them, her beady eyes gleaming. She swung her neck like a snake and let out a vicious snarl.

*Thump . . . thump . . . thump*. The angry dilophosaurus stomped forwards, her head outstretched and her gaze fixed hungrily on the babies. Then suddenly there was a furious roar and another dinosaur burst in front of them, her thick tail swishing from side to side. Rosie!

The dilophosaurus hissed, jerking her
head and puffing up her neck angrily. The
two adult dinosaurs circled each other.

Rosie herded her babies closer to the swamp, using her body to shield them. As they reached the edge she gave them each a quick nudge with her nose and they jumped in.

The dilophosaurus threw her head back and snarled.

But Rosie wasn't scared. She gave a loud, angry bellow that seemed to come from deep inside her tummy. Then she charged. Swishing her tail from side to side, she whipped out at the dilophosaurus. With a roar of pain as Rosie's tail hit her, the dilophosaurus staggered back. She roared again and, for a moment, it looked as though she was going to attack back, but Rosie lowered her head and charged once more. The dilophosaurus leaped out of the way of Rosie's horns.

'Rosie's winning!' Max cried.

As Rosie lumbered round for a third attempt, the dilophosaurus started to back away slowly.

'She's giving up!' exclaimed Fern.

They watched in excitement as the dilophosaurus took one last look at Rosie charging towards her, then turned and ran away.

# On the Mend!

'It's a miracle!' Fern cried, hurrying out of the house with Max as the dilophosaurus ran back to the wild.

They watched the baby dinosaurs rolling and splashing around in the swamp, having great fun. Satisfied that her little ones were safe, Rosie padded back to her enclosure.

Max looked thoughtful. 'Hang on! I've had an idea! Maybe if we can keep Cory in there with the baby triceratops for a while, Rosie will think he's one of hers when they come out!'

'But why would she think that?' asked Fern, puzzled. 'He looks different.'

'Yes, but I think it's supposed to be the smell that's important, not what the baby looks like. I remember my mum and dad talking – they said that the calf needed to smell right to the cow before she would see it as one of her own and foster it. If Cory stays in the swamp for long enough, he'll start to smell just the same as the others. After all, they'll all be smelling of the old swamp water.'

'Oh, I hope it works!' breathed Fern.

'If any of them try to get out, don't use your hands to put them back. It might put your scent on the babies,' said Max.

Fern nodded and they hurried over.

Whenever any of the baby dinosaurs tried to lift themselves on to solid ground, they gently eased them back in using reeds from around the swamp.

After a while, Fern nodded over her shoulder. 'Look, Rosie's coming back! We'd better get out of her way.'

They went to the side to watch. Max bit his lip. Would his plan work? He held his breath as they waited.

Rosie reached the swamp and bent down

to nuzzle her babies. She didn't seem upset to see Cory with them. Gently, she lifted out one baby triceratops by the scruff of its neck and placed it on the side. Then she helped the second one out in the same way.

So, her two real babies were safe. What would Rosie do now? She turned and . . .

Max punched the air with his fist as Rosie lifted Cory out too, just as if he was one of her own!

She nuzzled him gently before putting

him down beside the two baby triceratops.

'You were right, Max . . . you were right!'

Fern jumped up and down happily.

'Well, well, well,' said a man's voice.

'Who would have thought it. Amazing!'

Max turned and saw Adam coming over to join them as Rosie started to lead the three pups off to her enclosure.

Adam shook his head. 'That's not to say that what you two did was right,' he said, looking around him. 'We've got some broken fences to mend, and although no immediate harm's been done, you could have got us – and the dinosaurs here – killed!'

'But look, Dad, look,' Fern pointed out. 'Cory's going to be just fine.'

Max, Fern and her dad watched as the mother triceratops nuzzled the three pups.

'Hmm.' Adam still looked worried. 'I know things look OK just now, but what's going to happen when the swamp water wears off? We could be back to square one. And if Rosie rejects Cory a second time, it could be the end for him.'

Max looked at Fern as Adam's words rang in his ears. It was true, of course. He racked his brain. 'Perhaps we could help out,'

he said suddenly. 'We could keep covering
Cory with swamp water to hide his smell
until Rosie gets used to having three pups.
I remember Mum and Dad saying that with
foster cows the first few hours after the

cow has bonded with the new calf are the important ones. I think it will be the same for dinosaurs.'

'Brilliant!' said Adam, looking really impressed. 'You're full of good ideas, Max. All right, you two, you can be responsible for keeping Cory well-and-truly soaked while I clear up here. Let's give it a try!'

'Thanks, Dad,' said Fern, giving her dad a big hug. 'We won't let you down . . . I promise!'

Max and Fern spent the next few hours going back and forth with wooden pails of swampy water. It was thirsty and tiring work but a lot of fun too.

'Do you think it's working?' asked Fern as she poured another bucket over Cory.

'I don't know,' said Max, peeking in at the little dinosaur. Fern crept up behind him.

'Hey!' Max cried, as she splashed cold water all over him too.

Quickly, Max threw a handful of water

back, and in no time they were having a

water fight! They chased each other around

the pen giggling.

'All right, all right. I give in!' Max panted

finally. 'Stop! Stop! You win!' He flopped

down on to the ground. Fern came over to

join him but, just at that moment, there was

a little cry from Cory. Max and Fern leaped

to their feet. But they needn't have worried.

As they looked in, they could see that Rosie

was still nuzzling her new addition.

'We've been watering for ages,' Max said

as he watched Rosie snuffle around Cory.

'Do you think we've done enough?'

'I don't know,' said Fern. Just then her

dad came striding up to the pen.

'Hey, you two,' he called. 'Why don't you take a break? Looks like Cory's doing just fine. Come inside and have some food and we'll see how Rosie and Cory are after the swamp water dries.'

'All right, Dad,' said Fern. 'Just give us one last go.'

'OK,' said Adam with a smile, then he turned back to the house.

Fern and Max gave Cory one last soaking. They didn't really want to leave him but they knew Adam was right. They had done everything they could and they needed something to eat.

'Do you think it'll be OK?' said Fern as they headed back inside.

'I don't know.' Max swallowed hard. 'But I really hope so!'

# Back Home

Max and Fern had a supper of fresh bread and delicious creamy cheese in the stone house. It was good to sit down after all their hard work but they both felt anxious about what was happening with the dinosaurs outside.

As soon as they had finished their food

they were up, as quick as a flash, and rushing back outside.

They raced down the path and turned the corner to Rosie's enclosure. Max's heart skipped a beat, but then he let out a relieved sigh. One . . . two . . . three pups, all looking as contented as when they'd left them, were snuggled up into Rosie's broad sides. Cory looked very different from the others but Rosie was treating him just like her real babies. Cory gave a contented snort and cuddled closer to his new mum.

'Isn't it great?' cried Fern, her eyes shining. 'Look how happy Cory seems!'

'Your idea worked.' Adam came up behind them and laid a hand on Max's shoulder. 'I really can't thank you enough, Max. I thought Fern and I knew everything there was to know about dinosaurs but you've really taught us a thing or two today! I'm very glad the magic brought you here.'

Max smiled as he looked into Adam's

grateful brown eyes and he felt his chest puff up proudly.

'I'm glad too!' Fern hugged him.

Looking at the baby dinosaurs, Max felt happier than he had ever felt in his life. He'd had an amazing adventure and Cory had a family now. Max felt a lump rise in his throat as he wondered about his own family. It seemed like ages since he'd seen his mum and dad.

Suddenly he felt a tingling, red-hot sensation in his pocket. The fossil!

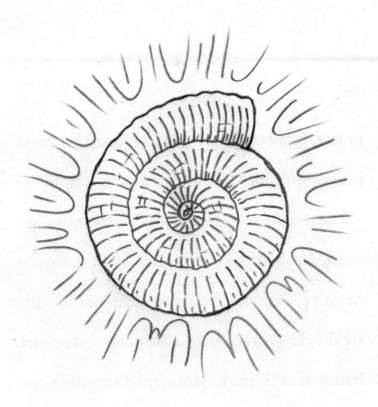

'I think the fossil is taking me home!'
Max cried, feeling excited as a rush of air
whooshed around him. Then he had an
awful thought. 'What if I don't ever see you
again?' he called.

'Oh, I have a feeling you will,' laughed Adam. 'I think that must be why the fossil brought you to us – because it knew we needed your help!'

'But . . . but . . .' Max was being lifted high into the air, spinning and whirling in a sea of colours. There was only just enough time to shout his farewells.

'Bye, Fern! Bye, Adam!' he called.

Max landed with a bump, and rubbed his eyes. It was dark and, for a moment, he thought he was in the little stone house in Dinosaur Land. Then his hand reached out and the warm, comforting feel of his duvet told him he was safely back home. His book lay on the bed, just as he had left it. *Phew*, Max thought – it looked as though no time had passed in the human world at all. Through a crack in the door, his mum's face appeared.

'Is that you, Max?' she said coming into the room. 'I thought I could hear you rustling the duvet. Now, come on, it really

is bedtime.'

Drawing up the cover, she placed a kiss

on his cheek. 'What's that you've got there?'

she asked, feeling under the cover. 'Not that

fossil again!' She laughed. 'Here. Let me put

it away for you.' She took the stone from

Max, turning it over in her hand before

placing it back on the shelf.

'It really is a beauty, isn't it?' she said.

'Not just a beauty,' Max murmured to

himself. 'It's magic too.'

'What was that, Max?' his mum said as she headed for the door.

'Oh, nothing, Mum,' said Max. 'I was just talking to myself.'

Max looked up at the fossil and smiled. He wondered what help Fern and Adam would need next time in Dinosaur Land. One thing was for sure . . . he couldn't wait to go there again!